WHEN MOMMY GOES TO WORK

Written by Dina Templeton

Illustrated by Anthony Sclavi

Clifton Carriage House
12 South Sixth Street No. 1250
Minneapolis, Minnesota 55402

10 9 8 7 6 5 4 3 2 1

Written by Dina Templeton
Illustrated and Designed by Anthony Sclavi

Type is set in Kitsu, One Stroke Script. Illustrations done in Dr. P.H. Martin's Concentrated Watercolor, Prismacolor felt pen and Mars Lumograph 8B pencil on 140 lb cold press watercolor paper.

Printed in the United States of America

International Standard Book Number 13: 978-0-9825713-5-4

Library of Congress Control Number: 2010915395
Registration No. Tux 1-680-539

First Edition

For Billy & Darla, the answer to my prayers - D.T.

To Rebecca and Rocco - A.S.

What does mommy do when mommy goes to work?

Does she sit and read great giant books and study every page?

Does she gather logs for firewood
then cut them with a saw?

Does she check all types of instruments to make sure they're in tune?

Does she put the fuel in rocket ships so they can fly up to the moon?

Does she lead a sparkling
marching band while swinging
a baton?

Does she drive a double-decker bus and tell people to hop on?

Does she try to juggle
watermelons with skates
upon her feet?

There are so many choices but which one can it be?

What is my mommy doing when mommy's not with me?

So you want to know what mommy does while you laugh and sing and play?

You want to know what mommy does while mommy is away?

This book is given with love to

_____

_____ / _____ / _____